TOM MBOYA

MASTER OF
MASS MANAGEMENT

BY
J. E. SIBI-OKUMU

an imprint of

PUBLISHERS
expanding minds

Published by **Sasa Sema** Publications
An imprint of Longhorn Publishers

Longhorn Kenya Ltd.,
Funzi Road, Industrial Area,
P.O. Box 18033-00500,
Nairobi, Kenya.

Longhorn Uganda Ltd.,
Plot M220, Ntinda Industrial Area.,
Jinja Road, P.O. Box 24745,
Kampala, Uganda.

Longhorn Publishers (T) Ltd.,
Msasani Village, Block F, House No. 664,
Old Bagamoyo Road,
Dar es Salaam, Tanzania.

Cover Design by ....

Illustrations by Clive Kamala Jerry

ISBN **978 9966 36 328 9**

Printed by Colourprint Ltd.,
Road C, off Enterprise Road
Behind Sameer Industrial Park
P.O. Box 44466 - 00100, Nairobi, Kenya

DEDICATION

For J and J

OTHER LION BOOKS

TABLE OF CONTENTS

PREFACE

Anyone interested in the history of Kenya should know something about Tom Mboya. A highly intelligent and charismatic man, he was an influential figure in the build-up to and the aftermath of the country's independence.

It goes without saying that, given his stature and contribution, much information of many kinds was available to me. I do not believe that a long academic list is called for in the circumstances. My aim, with the young reader in mind, was to encompass, to enlighten, to educate and to entertain, albeit in a challenging manner.

I am extremely grateful to the people who helped me along the way. As a teacher, I received much advice and encouragement from professional colleagues. I would like to thank, in particular, Tom Mboya's wife Pamela; his sister, Regina, his contemporary and friend William Wamalwa and film maker Salim Amin and his family, who all very kindly agreed to be part of the story, featuring as themselves. Special recognition must also go to my wife, Kaari Njeru, for her help with research and for keyboarding the first draft manuscript.

It has been a sentimental privilege for me to evoke the life and times of a man who was known to my parents and who was "Uncle Tom" to me as a young boy, as a result - with a picture in the family album to prove it - and about whom I remember writing a prize-winning essay for a competition in high school, all those years ago.

I do hope that with this book, my young readers will be continuing a lifelong love of language, an instrument of great possibility and pleasure.

John Sibi- Okumu.
14th May, 2008

CHAPTER ONE

THE STREET NAMES PROJECT:
HOW IT ALL BEGAN

"Now that we've got enough facts together, we'd better put them into some sort of order," Wanjiku said to Lengai. "Otherwise, we won't meet the deadline."

"This project has been so much fun!" Lengai replied. "At the beginning, I didn't imagine that our investigations would lead us in so many different directions. Who knows? I might just decide to become a real researcher when I grow up."

It was one of Miss Ahmed's famous **Truly Exciting Projects**. That is what she herself called them. Whether you agreed with her or not was an entirely different matter. The fact is, each one was almost always introduced with the same old words:

"Guess what, people? I have a truly exciting project for you. You're going to love it!"

They had done many before. Miss Soraya Ahmed, their class teacher, didn't believe in remembering facts off by heart, simply from having read them in a book.

"Learning is discovery and there's joy in that discovery. If at first you don't know; ask, ask and ask again. Find out for yourself!" Miss Ahmed would insist.

She came out with so many words of wisdom on any given day that they could have made up a book of their own. But there was no denying some things: she knew a lot. She was firm, yet fair. She was patient and she was kind. She could be very humourous, too. In short, Miss Ahmed was "really cool," in the language of her pupils. This time round, it all began on a Monday morning in a history lesson.

"People," she began.

She was always calling everybody *people*.

"As you move around Nairobi, your very own capital city, do you ever stop to ask yourself after whom all those streets were named?" Miss Ahmed always insisted that the students should *try* to speak grammatically correct English. You'd never hear her say "who those streets were named after." To her, that was not *good* English.

On the classroom wall, beside her blackboard, was a large poster with words she had typed up in big, bold letters. It read:

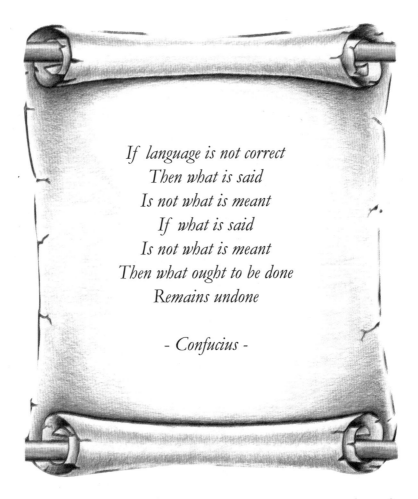

If language is not correct
Then what is said
Is not what is meant
If what is said
Is not what is meant
Then what ought to be done
Remains undone

- Confucius -

"Muindi Mbingu, David Osieli, Koinange, Wabera and Argwings Kodhek? Who were these people?" she asked.

"And what part did they play in Kenya's history to deserve such an honour?"

Not a single hand went up.

"Well, people, guess what?" Miss Ahmed continued.

"I have a truly exciting project for you! You're going to love it!"

Knowing smiles spread across the classroom. The children waited for the familiar instructions.

"Since you know I like you to work with a different person each time, I've worked out some new partners. Remember it's always best to work as a team. Why T.E.A.M?"

The whole class replied in unison:

"Because Together Everyone Achieves More!"

"You're right!" Miss Ahmed agreed.

"Knowing you as I do, I've tried to find a good reason to place a particular person in a particular group. This time, each group will comprise two members only."

Miss Ahmed went on to read out from her list. That's how Wanjiku and Lengai got to work together.

"Wanjiku Otieno and Lengai Kipkemboi, as all your parents are from different parts of the country, the man I want you to research on was brought up among people from every part of Kenya. He felt at home with them all and could speak several local languages. Any offers?" Not a single hand went up.

"His name was Tom Mboya," Miss Ahmed declared.

"Once again, you will have to prepare presentations and creative displays which will first be shown in the school library before we find space to stick some up on the classroom wall. As usual, for each group, I have put together a useful information envelope with source materials, guiding questions, a mark scheme and suggestions on how to proceed. Source materials could be either quotations or pictures or cartoons or maps or newspaper headlines." Wanjiku raised her hand.

"Yes, Wanjiku."

"Are we allowed to use the Internet, Miss?"

"A difficult question, Wanjiku. I wouldn't say no but I would advise you against it. Perhaps, you may use it as a guide. But there is so much information on the web, I think that you have to wait until you're a little bit older to know how to make head or tail of it and use it to your advantage. Plus, there is a huge temptation to download and photocopy huge chunks of material that you don't really understand. So, please make use of other research methods. Oops! There goes the bell! The rest is up to you. You have six weeks. Good luck, oh daring discoverers! Please pick up your information envelopes on your way out. Thank you, people!"

Another truly exciting project had begun.

CHAPTER TWO

FIRST THINGS FIRST:
CREATING A TIMELINE

O Key, Lengai. What have you got down for our timeline? I'll take your notes and you can leave it to me to draw it up at home." Wanjiku could be a little bossy at times, but she was a good partner because she could be relied upon to get things done. To fulfil his given task, Lengai had had gone to the **World History** and **African History** sections of the school library.

"Well, I settled on the year 1900 as a starting point: The beginning of the twentieth century. So we would have to note the two world wars, the first from 1914 to1918 and the second from 1939 to 1945.

Then I have some dates with the names of people who were somehow linked to the African continent:

- 1948, the death of Mahatma Ghandi in India.
- 1965, the death of the African American, Malcolm X.
- 1968, the death of Martin Luther King, Junior, also an African American. Thinking of America, I also put down.
- 1963, for the assassination of President John F. Kennedy and.
- 1969, when man first landed on the moon."

"Good!" Wanjiku said.

"But we'd better watch out. We could end up giving Miss Ahmed ideas for another truly exciting project at the end of all this!"

"Well that wouldn't be all that bad, would it? In fact, it could be quite cool. Here's what I've got on Africa in general:

- 1957, the year when Ghana became the first African nation to gain independence, with Kwame Nkrumah as president.
- 1960,1961and 1962, the years when many other African countries, including Uganda and Tanganyika, also became independent.
- 1963, the year Nelson Mandela began twenty

seven years of imprisonment on Robben Island in South Africa. As for this country in particular, at the beginning of the twentieth century, what is now Kenya was still under British colonial rule.

• In 1952, the colonialists declared a State of Emergency for eight years against the *Mau Mau,* a resistance movement. Kenya became independent in 1963, with Jomo Kenyatta, who died in 1978, as its first president." Wanjiku put in the obvious question:

"So, where does our man fit into all this?"

"Tom Mboya was born in 1930," came the confident reply from Lengai, "and died in 1969. He was only 39, you know. Our timeline could end in the year 2009, the fortieth anniversary of his death.

"Well done! Now, it's back to basics." She raised her right hand dramatically. "Let our quest for more knowledge begin. May I declare this research project on Tom Mboya officially started!" Then, just as dramatically, she brought down her right hand. "Here! Here!" Lengai responded, in agreement.

CHAPTER THREE

FROM SISAL FIELDS
TO SEMINARY:
YOUNG TOM GOES TO SCHOOL

My parents know Pamela Mboya, Mr Mboya's wife," Wanjiku revealed. "My father has phoned her, talked to her and arranged for us to go and see her! How's that for detective starters?"

"When shall we go?" Lengai asked.

"This weekend," Wanjiku replied. "If you come to our house at about ten on Saturday morning, then my dad will take us."

The awaited day eventually arrived. Lengai was dropped off at the Otienos' home in good time. Mr Odongo Otieno came from Bondo near Lake Victoria in Western Kenya. At about ten thirty, he was sitting at the wheel of his car, ready to take the daring discoverers to Mrs Mboya's house.

"Now, future leaders," Mr Otieno began. He called every young person he met "future leader." This made the young people feel very important and special.

"Here's the plan. When we get there, I'll leave you two to get on with your research. I'll be back to fetch you in about half an hour. I hope you realise that she is doing you a very special favour. So, don't take up too much of her time and be sure to thank her when you leave."

"Okey," came the reply and off they went. Mr Otieno told them that Mrs Pamela Mboya lived in a block of flats in the heart of Nairobi. When they got there, Mr Otieno asked the security guard to take the children to the lift and to show them to Mrs Mboya's house. Mrs Mboya came to open the door herself. She was very tall, elegantly dressed and wore glasses.

"Hello, children," she said. "Do come in!"

The living room of her flat was quite spacious and tastefully furnished. There was a black and white picture of Mr Mboya on one wall.

There were also other pictures of her own children, all grown up now, either alone or with their families. The couple had had two sons and two daughters.

"Wanjiku, I've known your father and mother for a long time. Who is your friend?" she asked.

"Lengai Kipkemboi, Mrs Mboya."

"Oh, what a nice name. Where are your parents from, Lengai, if I may ask?"

"My father is from near Eldoret and my mother is from Kajiado," Lengai explained.

"Have your parents told you how they got to know each other?"

"Yes, they have. They told me they were high school sweethearts who first met at a debating competition and started writing letters to each other and then it all went from there."

"Oh, how romantic!" Mrs Mboya exclaimed.

"If only the whole of Kenya was such a mixture of origins as the two of you, we would be a truly united country! Welcome, Lengai."

"Thank you, Mrs Mboya," said Lengai in return.

"Let's go and sit on the balcony," Mrs Mboya continued.

"You're lucky, because my sister- in-law has come to visit. She's sitting there already and she can answer some of your questions, too. Only I'll have to ask them for you in Dholuo because her English and Kiswahili aren't very good."

They headed for the balcony through the dining room.

"You can say *Amosi*! when you meet her. It means hello," Wanjiku whispered to Lengai, conspiratorially.

"That's right," said Mrs Mboya, who overheard her.

Mrs Mboya's sister-in-law was introduced as Regina. She nodded and smiled. Wanjiku and

Lengai threw quick glances at each other before saying, *"Amosi."*

"Ber ahinya," Regina replied, obviously delighted by this ice-breaking greeting. There were already enough chairs laid out for all of them to sit down. Mrs Mboya offered the children some orange juice, which they accepted. They both thanked her. It was in the conversation that followed that Wanjiku and Lengai learned about Tom Mboya's family life, luckily from two people who had actually been part of it. Regina, Tom Mboya's sister was an unexpected, extra source of information. Wanjiku and Lengai asked her questions in English, which Mrs Mboya translated into Dholuo. Regina answered in Dholuo and Mrs Mboya translated back into English for the children. It may sound very complicated but it worked.

Tom Mboya's parents, Leonardus Ndiege and Marcella Awuor originally came from Rusinga Island on Lake Victoria. Eventually,

Mr Mboya's father worked as a supervisor on a sisal plantation at a place called Kilimambogo, near Thika. That is where Mr Mboya himself was born on 15th August, 1930. He was the first of eight children in all, five boys and three girls. The plantation had other workers from different parts of Kenya. Therefore, from a very early age, Mr Mboya, his brothers and sisters learned to get along with children whose parents had come to work on the sisal farm from elsewhere. The young Mboya could communicate in several languages, including Kiswahili, Kikuyu and Kikamba, as well as Kisuba and Dholuo, that were first languages for his parents.

"Where did he go to school?" Lengai asked Regina.

"As a little boy, my brother first went to a school run by Catholic missionaries for two years. The missionaries introduced him to the Catholic religion and mainly taught him how to say his prayers. But our father realised how important a good education was. He sent Tom away to live with a friend of his at a place called Kabaa, amongst the Akamba people, so that he could go to a proper school. But it was very different from what you know as school. Tom and his fellow pupils sat in the shade of trees for their lessons. They wrote in the sand with sticks because they had no books and pens." Regina went on with her description:

"In those days, people who could afford books and pens might have had a radio or a bicycle. In the evening people ate, talked among themselves by the light of a kerosene lamp, got ready for the next day and went to sleep. No one had tap water. No one had indoor toilets. We had no household electricity."

Wanjiku and Lengai realised that this meant no telephones, no television, no videos, no CD's, no ipods, no computer games like Playstation.

They found it very difficult to imagine.

"So, what games did children play?"

"Oh, lots! We spent lots of time outside in the fresh air. Nobody had to tell us to get up and exercise. Life was safer for children. We ran about, all over the place. And we made our own, simple but enjoyable toys. We played hopscotch. Boys made footballs out of old bits of cloth. They made catapults and went hunting."

"Children belonged to every adult, not just to their own parents. If we were hungry, we were given something to eat wherever we happened to be. And it was good, healthy food. Grown-ups told us stories. We were taught songs, under the moonlight, before we went to sleep. I think those days are gone, forever."

"Wow!" Lengai responded. "That's cool!"

Regina continued the story about her brother's childhood.

"So, Tom learned to read and write. He then moved to a boarding school called St Mary's in Yala, many miles away, in Western Kenya. It was also a seminary, a place meant to prepare whoever went there to eventually become a Catholic priest. During some holidays, Tom stayed on to work as a cook for his teachers, in order to earn some money. After finishing primary school at Yala, Tom decided that he didn't want to become a priest and returned to central Kenya. He went to the famous Mangu School near Thika, which was to produce many of Kenya's future leaders."

"In those days, students sat for a national examination after the first two years in high school. Tom passed it very well but our father could not afford the fees for him to continue secondary education. That's when he started a course at the medical school in Kabete, just outside Nairobi. In the end, he got a job as a health inspector, making sure that Nairobi was a clean place to live in."

Wanjiku had a question for Regina:

"How comes you didn't go to school like your brother?"

"Well, very, very few families sent girls to school. They didn't think that it was of any use since girls could only be wives and mothers. Times have changed a lot, I'm glad to say. I was very envious of my big brother. He went far away. He spent time in the big town of Nairobi, with its tall buildings, its many shops, its cars and buses. I remember the smart uniforms he wore, especially the one he had as a health inspector, complete with stockings and shiny shoes. The rest of us walked barefoot when we were little. I thought my brother was very handsome. And he was always so well dressed.

21

"Tom was a born leader. At primary and secondary school he was made a prefect. At the medical school, he was president of the Students' Council. And as a health inspector, he was chosen to represent his fellow workers. As the years passed, I heard that Tom was becoming well known for organising workers into unions so that, together, they could ask for better conditions of work and pay. Without being afraid of what would happen to him, he stood before hundreds of people and persuaded them to go on strike. But this would only be as a last resort, because he believed firmly in solving problems through negotiation.

"I couldn't believe it when I was told that he was flying all over the world, in an aeroplane.

We used to wave at the airplanes, thinking that he might be in one of them either; leaving or coming back home. He went for further studies at Oxford University, then to Ghana for discussions to try to create a united Africa, then to America, then back to England to prepare for our *Uhuru*. And our Tom wasn't selfish. He helped lots of other young Kenyans to go to America to study. And then there he was, a minister in the government! Always planning, always organising. Tom was a wonderful speaker, capable of bringing people together from all parts of the country. Who wouldn't be proud of a brother like that?"

"Could you please tell us what he did in his spare time?" Lengai asked Mrs Mboya.

"Tom loved to read. He read all the time. He also loved to sing. He learned to play the guitar and was always composing songs. Oh yes! And he loved dancing. Tom was simply the best dancer around. He was an avid photographer, as well. He was very fond of our children and he loved to come home and play with them. On weekends, he and the children would go on long drives and he would take lots and lots of pictures."

"When did you get married?" Lengai asked, again.

"Tom and I were married at a huge wedding ceremony in January, 1962. He was thirty-one. I was much younger than he was. I must tell you that he had been married before and had had two daughters with his first wife. But that marriage fell apart. Our wedding was attended by many well-known guests. VIP's or Very Important People, as they're called. We can go back into the living room and I'll show you some pictures."

Wanjiku and Lengai thanked Regina. Wanjiku knew how to say it in Dholuo and Regina smiled approvingly when she heard: *"Ero Kamano!"*

There were lots of lovely pictures in the photo album. Wanjiku and Lengai could tell that it had been a huge ceremony. The pictures recorded such happy moments that neither of the children could pluck up the courage to ask Mrs Mboya about her husband's death.

As they were about to leave, Mrs Mboya went to the mantlepiece and picked up a small box which she offered to Wanjiku.

"Here are two cassettes. I have copied recordings of some speeches that my husband made. You can ask your parents to let you listen to them at home. I bet you didn't know that,

before independence, he was featured on the
front cover of 'Time,' the international magazine
published in the USA?"

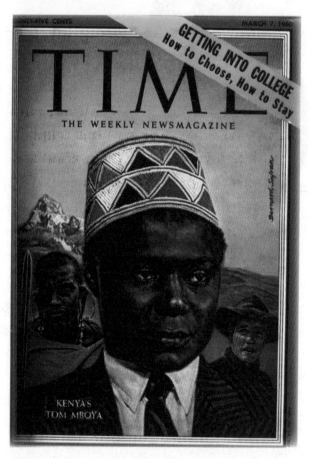

"No, we didn't," Wanjiku admitted.

"You see," Mrs Mboya explained, "it was
quite something for Time magazine to have an
African on its front cover. This was proof that

others, outside Kenya, recognised leadership qualities in Tom that made him stand out on the whole continent."

The children couldn't believe their luck. They needed no reminder to express their appreciation.

"Thank you very much for your time, Mrs Mboya," Wanjiku said.

"And for your kind gift," Lengai added. They could see the bonus marks piling up for their presentation in class.

CHAPTER FOUR

MARSHALLING MORE MATERIAL:
ASKING, ASKING AND ASKING AGAIN

After the visit to Mrs Mboya, Lengai went back to the Otienos' house for lunch so that he and Wanjiku could continue to work in the afternoon. They decided to begin listening to one of the cassettes that Mrs Mboya had given them on the Otienos' stereo system. They were able to hear what Tom Mboya sounded like for the first time. Miss Ahmed would have loved the way that he spoke *good* English: clearly, distinctly, with correct grammar and a large vocabulary.

"Wow!" Lengai said. "If you take away the slight accent, you'd almost think that he was a well educated Englishman!"

"Yes," Wanjiku agreed.

"He must have read and written a lot on his own. As Miss Ahmed says, if you want to be really good at something you must be prepared to spend a lot of time getting good at it. Practice makes perfect. And always remember: a reader is a leader."

They particularly noted Mr Mboya's words on the subject of national unity:

"We are fortunate that we have enjoyed nearly two years of independence with relative harmony, peace and stability. And that gradually we are moving towards a united nation. The tribal feelings have gradually disappeared and the racial anxieties are also disappearing, and in many cases, have disappeared. But I choose to speak about this subject today because, as I have just said, unity is not something that we can take for granted. Nor can we now, just because we have had two years of relative peace and harmony, assume that this will always be so. Unless our leaders and our people continue to exercise the same vigilance and understanding that is necessary to promote unity in our nation, there is a danger that because we have enjoyed this harmony and unity in this country, some people are likely to forget that the future lies in a united Kenyan nation. And that we cannot talk of building a nation if we cannot succeed in creating national unity and understanding."

Lengai had a suggestion: "You know on our timeline we had Kenya's independence day and the year Tom Mboya died? Why not interview your parents about what they remember about those dates? One for each...."

"Okay. Although we had better catch my dad before he settles down to watch football on TV. It's a lost cause trying to talk to him after that."

Mr Otieno was indeed in the sitting room, but reading the newspaper.

"Dad. May we disturb you for a moment?" Wanjiku asked.

"Yes, of course. It's about your project, isn't it?"

"Yes, dad," Wanjiku replied.

"Well, as long as you promise to mention me by name as a hero when you make your presentation." Wanjiku and Lengai laughed. Mr Otieno could be so funny, at times.

"Okay, dad. Promised! Where were you on independence day?"

"I was at our home in Nairobi, South B," Mr Otieno began. "However, it was a special day for us as children, too. I shall never forget it. For one thing, my mother made a delicious lunch of chicken with rice and *chapatis*. My sister and I were

made to sleep in the afternoon so that we would
be awake late at night to watch the ceremony on

T.V. In those days, there were no colour T.Vs.
The screen was tiny and the reception wasn't that
good at times but we could see that there were
hundreds of people at the stadium. I was seven
at the time so I don't remember much. But I do
remember that, just before midnight, the screen
went dark. When there was a clear image again,
the new Kenyan flag, black, green, red and white,
was flying instead of the British Union Jack. Then
absolutely magical fireworks lit up the evening sky.
Everyone went wild. It was absolutely fantastic!"

"You don't remember seeing Mr Mboya, do you?" Lengai asked.

"Now, that I don't remember, to tell you the truth. But he was definitely there! Great organiser that he was, I'm sure that much of what we were seeing was courtesy of him."

"Thanks, dad," said Wanjiku. "We are going to put our other question to mum so that she can get to be a heroine."

Mrs Wairimu Otieno came from Kiambu in Central Province. She had first met her husband when both were at the University of Nairobi. Now she was in the study room, preparing for work on Monday.

"Mum, where were you when Mr Mboya was shot?" Wanjiku asked.

"I was at the showground in Kisumu. It was a Saturday, the last day of the annual Kisumu Agricultural Fair. My parents had taken my sister, my brother and I there. They left us to wander around on our own, visiting the various stands while they sat with friends in the Members' Club.

"My father had been to America on one of the airlifts that Mr Mboya helped to organise. He studied Agriculture at the University of South Dakota. When he returned, the colonialists were no longer in power. Kenyatta's government employed him in the Ministry of Agriculture. Every two years, the Ministry would post him to different parts of the country to teach farmers how to use their land as best as possible. That's how we happened to be in Kisumu in 1969. I was ten years old. I remember feeling quite helpless in the big crowd. In the early afternoon, a voice came through on a loudspeaker. It said that an important announcement had to be made. There had just been a news flash on the radio. Tom Mboya had been shot in Nairobi! He had been rushed to hospital. You should have seen the reaction!

"People began to weep uncontrollably. Some began singing, singing very sorrowful songs. Some cut branches off the trees and started waving them from side to side, singing and chanting, all the while. Sometime later, the same voice from the loudspeaker made another announcement. There had been a second news flash: Tom Mboya was dead!

"You cannot imagine the chaos that erupted. It was frightening. For me, the crowd seemed to have grown even bigger and angrier. There were people running about, all over the place, shrieking, wailing, pulling at their hair, waving even more branches. Some picked up and threw stones in their anger. The police were incapable of keeping order. Somehow we managed to get out of the showground.

"I don't remember how we linked up with my mother and father. All I remember was the look on my father's face as he drove us back home. No one in the car spoke except him. He was mumbling to himself: 'I can't believe it! How could they do that? Tom is dead! Tom is dead!'"

"Wow!" Lengai exclaimed. "I can't imagine it. It's so scary."

"It was scary, I can tell you," Mrs Otieno continued.

How's he project going, generally?"

"Not bad," Lengai explained.

"We're doing quite well on Mr Mboya's private life but there are still big gaps on the public man."

"Well, a visit to some libraries would help," Mrs Otieno suggested. "We could arrange that in the next few weekends. And, also, the major newspapers store past copies, either as they were first printed, which can be photocopied or, more and more these days, on something called micro-film."

"What's that, mum?" Wanjiku asked.

"Pictures are taken of the actual newspaper and the pages are filed as very light negatives which can be viewed through a projector. The only problem is that they won't allow children your age to go in and look at them."

"I know what!" Lengai exclaimed. "I'll ask my big brother, Kibet, to help us. He's at the University of Nairobi and he would be allowed into all these places. I'm sure there's a university library as well."

"There is indeed, Lengai," said Mrs Otieno.

"Not bad thinking for a boy!" Wanjiku interjected.

"Now, now, Wanjiku," her mother chided. "There is no need for sarcasm. That's very good thinking, Lengai. I hope that he agrees. It seems to me that both of you are on the way to a first class project. The best of luck to you."

When Mr Otieno and Wanjiku dropped off Lengai at home, his mother, who worked in an advertising agency, had another good idea for them:

"I think I can arrange for you to see Mr Salim Amin. His father, Mohamed Amin took exclusive pictures of Mr Mboya's final moments. Mo, as he was popularly known, became a world famous Kenyan before he died. Salim took over from his father and is in charge of one of the largest film libraries in Kenya as head of a company called Camerapix, here in Nairobi."

"Cool, mum," Lengai said. "Really cool. If at first you don't know; ask, ask and ask again!"

"Correct!" his mother agreed.

CHAPTER FIVE

THE IMPORTANCE OF KEEPING RECORDS:

MR AMIN SHINES A LIGHT ON THE PAST

T he following weekend, it was Mrs Somoine Kipkemboi's turn to act as chauffeur to the daring discoverers. The Camerapix offices and Mr Salim Amin's own house were on the same compound in a part of Nairobi called Lavington. At the gate, a security guard asked Mrs Kipkemboi to sign herself in by giving various details. She did so but explained that she herself was not going to stay.

"Please tell Mr Amin that we're here. He is expecting us."

The guard made a phone call. Very soon thereafter, the children could see a very tall, very big, bespectacled man with a moustache approaching their car.

"Hi, Somoine!" he said to Mrs Kipkemboi. "Good to see you, again."

"Hi, Salim. It's very good of you to do this."

"My pleasure," Mr Amin reassured.

"Anything to be of help." Some introductions followed.

"Well then, I'll leave you to it," Mrs Kipkemboi said. "An hour or so will do, won't it?"

"Perhaps an hour and a half. I've set up a documentary film on the road to Kenya's independence. Then we can look at a photo tribute my father made to Tom, have a little chat and I am sure my girls will want to play a little. I'll give you a ring, don't worry."

In the main house, Wanjiku and Lengai met Mr Amin's wife Farzana and the couple's young daughters Saher and Saaniye.

They sipped orange juice as they watched the film in a TV room.

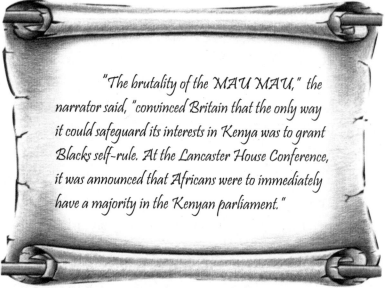

"The brutality of the MAU MAU," the narrator said, "convinced Britain that the only way it could safeguard its interests in Kenya was to grant Blacks self-rule. At the Lancaster House Conference, it was announced that Africans were to immediately have a majority in the Kenyan parliament."

Then Tom Mboya came on:

" I believe that one day Kenya will be governed by a democratic government, representative and elected by the people," he was heard to say. "And by the people, I include anybody who decides to make Kenya his home, and who accepts to be treated as an equal citizen with everybody else."

"I think he is as cute as a Teddy Bear," Wanjiku whispered to Lengai.

Tom Mboya appeared again, several times. Further on, they saw images of the independence celebrations, of the new Kenya flag being raised and of VIPs dancing "the twist," which they found quite funny. At the end of the film, Mr Amin came into the room and asked them about their impressions of Tom Mboya. Lengai was the first to respond.

"Well you could see that, because he spoke so well, he was called upon to speak for and on behalf of others."

"Yes," Mr Amin agreed. "Tom Mboya was definitely full of charisma."

"Could you please explain what that means?" Wanjiku enquired.

"Well to have charisma, to be charismatic, is to stand out effortlessly in a crowd so that nobody can ignore you."

"Thank you," Wanjiku said.

"Take a look at this photographic tribute that my father put together," Mr Amin offered.

Wanjiku and Lengai positioned themselves to look at a book of black and white pictures, some of which they had already seen at Mrs Mboya's flat. But here also, they could see the pictures of the unconscious Mboya in an ambulance, with tubes plugged into his nose, on the way to hospital. It made the children sad to look at them.

"He was shot, wasn't he?" Wanjiku advanced. "Do people know who did it, Mr Amin?"

"To tell you the truth, mystery still surrounds the exact circumstances of Tom Mboya's death. A man called Nahashon Njenga Njoroge was arrested and accused of the murder. He was finally sentenced to death by hanging, but he insisted that he had not acted alone." Wanjiku made a note of the name.

"Thank you, Mr Amin. Thanks for the film and the pictures. We have more or less put all the pieces together."

"Yes, thank you, Sir," Lengai added.

"It's a pleasure to meet such polite young people who are also thirsty for knowledge." Mr Amin said.

"Now, let me call your mum to come and fetch you. In the meantime, why don't you link up with the girls and keep them company for a while. They'll like that. All work and no play makes Jack a dull boy. Do you know that English proverb? "

"Yes," Lengai replied. "But work was interesting that it didn't seem like work at all."

"That's exactly as it should be. Another saying is that you should make your vocation your vacation!"

CHAPTER SIX

GUNSHOTS IN THE AFTERNOON SUN:
HOW TOM MBOYA MET HIS END

T he children had met Mrs Mboya and Regina, her sister-in-law. Salim Amin had shown them historic pictures and a film footage at Camerapix. And Lengai's brother, Kibet, had done them a favour by getting photocopies of newspaper articles at the time. Now, it was time for Wanjiku and Lengai to start being creative, as required for their displays. They split the work between themselves, working as a team to achieve more. Lengai took it upon himself to recreate, with words, the scene of Tom Mboya's death. This is what he wrote:

In Loving Memory of
Thomas J. Odhiambo Mboya

The date: Saturday, the 5th July, 1969.

The place: Nairobi, Kenya.

The time:? Early afternoon:

It was a lovely day. A well dressed man, an African, almost exactly a month short of becoming thirty nine years old, parked his car along a street called Government Road. He made his way to Chhani's, his usual pharmacist's shop. He went inside. The owners knew him well and greeted him fondly. He bought some skin cream. He opened the door to leave. Suddenly, two loud noises cut through the air. Gunshots! All of a sudden, all was confusion. A bullet ripped through the man's heart. Another hit him in the shoulder. Some people rushed to help him.

He had difficulty in breathing. He became unconscious. An ambulance arrived. He was taken to a nearby hospital. A photographer, Mohamed Amin, who recognised him as a minister in the Kenyan government, was taking pictures all the time and got into the ambulance as well. By the time they got to the hospital, the man was dead. Today, a road very close to where he was shot is named after him. To many, he was known simply as "Tom." His full name was Thomas Joseph Odhiambo Mboya.

As for Wanjiku, inspired by her grandfather's experience at university in the United States, she imagined how the news from Kenya might have been reported in an American newspaper. She typed her presentation on her father's computer. This was her offering for a creative display:

THE SOUTH DAKOTA STAR

No. 1234   Saturday, 12th July, 1969   Price 10 cents

Slain Kenyan Politician Buried

Politician Thomas Joseph Mboya was yesterday buried amidst scenes of great sadness at the family home on Rusinga Island in Western Kenya, six days after he fell to an assassin's bullet.

Since last Sunday, when his body was taken to his house in Lavington, Nairobi for public viewing, tears, anger and disbelief have marked his final journey. Police had to use tear gas to disperse rioting mourners at the Holy Family Catholic Cathedral on Tuesday, 8th July.

The following day Mboya's body set off on the slow journey by car to its final resting place. Huge, grief stricken crowds lined the route. Mboya's death has sparked off the divisive tensions that he himself always urged against in his public sayings.

Tom Mboya was a key player in Kenya's struggle for independence from British colonial rule. In recent times, there has been much competition to find a successor to the ageing President Jomo Kenyatta. Once again, the demon of division has reared his ugly head.

Mboya, a young and charismatic man with obvious ambition, was already a powerful minister in the government and major contender for greater political power. He was a superb orator, with many followers nationally. His enemies, convinced of his influence, must have concluded that the only way to stop him was to kill him. The search is on for those who did the dirty deed.

Meanwhile, Kenya is in the grip of its most dramatic national crisis since independence from Britain on December 12th, 1963.

One thing cannot be denied: When the history books are written, Tom Mboya is unlikely to be ignored. As he was being laid to rest for the last time, a gentle breeze was blowing across Lake Victoria. What was it the wind was wistfully whispering?

Perhaps that the lives of those who were truly great should never be forgotten. So might it be with Thomas Joseph Odhiambo Mboya.

CHAPTER SEVEN

THE FEELINGS OF A FRIEND:
A LONG CONVERSATION WITH MR WAMALWA

L engai's father, Mr Solomon Kipkemboi, led the daring discoverers to another person who had known Tom Mboya in real life. His name was Mr William Wamalwa and he lived in Karen, a suburb of Nairobi, in a large house with a lush garden, built on the edge of a forest. He was alone at home. Mr Wamalwa was one of the very first African Kenyans to receive a university education.

After Kenya became independent in 1963, he was appointed Clerk to the Cabinet. Whenever President Kenyatta met with all his ministers, it was one of Mr Wamalwa's duties to record what had been discussed and to see to it that decisions were followed up. He was, therefore, very much part of history in the making.

"However," Mr Kipkemboi warned. "Mr Wamalwa is likely to be biased in favour of Mr Mboya. Not only did they work together, but they were also friends. So, as good historians in future, you would have to check and confirm what he says by talking to people who didn't particularly like Mr Mboya to get another point of view."

In fact, that was one of the very first things that Mr Wamalwa brought up himself:

"I am very glad that you have come to see me," he said.

"It is always a pleasure to talk to young people like yourselves, the future leaders of our country and of our world. However, I must warn you beforehand that Mr Mboya was my friend. I still think that he was one of the most capable, intelligent, fearless, eloquent and articulate human beings that I have ever met."

Mr Wamalwa wore spectacles. He spoke very slowly and deliberately.

"I know I am in the presence of two brave researchers. So please stop me if, at any point, I am telling you what you know already."

"Do you mind if we tape record our conversation, as well as taking notes?" Wanjiku asked.

"Not at all," came the reply. "Where would you like me to begin?"

"Well, Sir, we know quite a lot about everything except his working life," Lengai explained.

"Fair enough," Mr Wamalwa responded. Wanjiku switched the tape recorder on. "I think I am right in saying that, having left Mangu, Tom started working in 1951, at the age of twenty one, as a health inspector, a job that required him to help keep the city of Nairobi biologically clean. A natural leader and organiser, he became interested in the working conditions of all African workers, like himself. Eventually, he was forced to give up his job in order to represent them. It was as a trade union leader or workers' representative

during the days of colonial rule that Mr Mboya first got the opportunity to travel abroad. In 1955, he flew to England, a rare thing for Africans in those days, to study about workers' rights at the Ruskin College of Oxford University."

"When he returned to Kenya, he continued to live amongst his fellow Africans in the part of Nairobi that was specifically set aside for them on the east side of the little town, as it was then. Europeans and Asians also lived in segregated or separate areas, elsewhere. All this was to change, of course, otherwise I wouldn't be living where I am now. Tom first acquired a national profile as a trade unionist but became more and more involved in politics. In 1957, he was one of the first Africans to be elected to the Legislative Council, the decision making body or parliament of the time."

"In 1958, in what he described in his autobiography, **'Freedom and After,'** as the proudest moment in his life, he was elected chairman of the first All Africa Peoples' Conference, hosted by Kwame Nkrumah in Accra, Ghana. But Tom was not just out for himself. He helped others as well. Between 1959 and 1963, he was instrumental in arranging what was called the Students' Airlifts to the USA, with the help of American friends who raised the money needed. When they returned home, many of these students became African pioneers in various spheres of life, the first to become what they had become.

"The airlifts allowed hundreds of students from East and Central Africa, who couldn't have afforded it otherwise, to go abroad for higher education.

"Tom Mboya took part in the discussions in London, at a place called Lancaster House, that led to Kenya's independence in 1963 and he helped to draw up the country's first constitution.

I hope that I am not talking down to you when I explain that a constitution is the system of laws that states the rights of the people and the powers of the government.

"There are two little known facts about Tom and our independence. For one, of all the submissions, it was he who made the ultimate choice of the tune that became our national anthem. And secondly, despite the approaching bad weather, it was he who ordered the mountaineers involved not to cancel their climb to hoist our national flag on top of Mount Kenya.

"For a year, quite apart from being an elected Member of Parliament for Bahati in Nairobi, with constituents from every corner of the land, Tom was Minister for Justice and Constitutional Affairs.

"From the end of 1964 to the time that he was killed, four and a half years later, he was in charge of the economy, the way the country managed its wealth, with the title Minister for Economic Planning and Development."

Then Mr Wamalwa said, "Gosh! I must stop doing all the talking. I am so sorry. Over to you, young people. Your questions, please. Who is going to set the ball rolling?"

Wanjiku and Lengai were really flattered that Mr Wamalwa was treating them so seriously and with such politeness, just as he would with adults. Wanjiku did not hesitate to go first.

"We know that he was an excellent public speaker, but what was Mr Mboya like, in private?"

"Well," Mr Wamalwa replied. "First of all, I must say that be it in public or in private, Tom stood out because of the way he looked and the way he spoke. Tom was very proud of his appearance. He was a very sharp dresser. His shoes were always polished to sparkling brightness. In matters of style, he was a role model for all young Kenyans. If they saw Tom in a velvet jacket, they went out and bought one too."

"Tom spoke without effort, without hesitation, but with conviction and often with lots of humour. He was very versatile intellectually. Whatever the subject, he could turn his mind with ease from agriculture, to education, to communication, to health and make you feel that he had spent his whole life thinking about each one. He not only had a good brain, he was a voracious reader and he was capable of great concentration. Tom was disciplined and worked very, very hard at everything he did."

It was Lengai's turn to ask a question: "Since he was so clever, was he a show-off?"

"I don't think that Tom was an arrogant man, as some people might claim. In fact, although he was able to address large crowds, I would say there was a part of his nature that was quite shy. However, I think it is also true to say that Tom could be impatient with poor thinking.

He liked ideas and serious debate and respected people who thought before they spoke." Wanjiku pursued the line of questioning:

"So did Mr Mboya always try to have his own way?"

"Hmm. I certainly have to think before answering your questions. You certainly are well prepared, young people! Let me see...... I think to state that he always wanted to impose his own will on other people would be slightly unfair to Tom. He was, quite simply, a very good organiser of people. He was good at it. In a nutshell, Tom Mboya was a master of mass management. For him, actions really spoke louder than words. Within KANU, the Kenyan African National Union, his own political party, President Kenyatta himself clearly recognised Tom's ability to tackle the most difficult problems and to produce ideas and solutions."

"Did his ideas and solutions have a good or bad effect on Kenya today?" Lengai pursued.

"Another very difficult question. Young people, it is so easy to make judgments with what is known as the wisdom of hindsight."

"Please explain," Lengai asked.

"The wisdom of hindsight," Mr Wamalwa

explained, "is when one looks back on an event after it has happened and feels well prepared to explain why it ought or ought not to have happened. May I ask if you like football?"

"Yes, lots!" Lengai answered.

"Well, young man," Mr Wamalwa continued, "it's like watching an action replay on TV in a football match and thinking that, if *you* had been there, you could easily have scored the missed goal. Does that make sense?"

"Yes," came the reply.

Since Mr Wamalwa seemed to take an interest in football himself, Lengai felt a great urge to ask him which team he supported. However, this was serious business and that would be for another visit, perhaps.

"So, with the wisdom of hindsight, it would be easy to either blame or give credit to Tom and others of my generation for the way things are today. What you must realise, young people, is that we were all responding to the moment and making what we thought were the best decisions at the time. We weren't fortune tellers. So, we did influence the future but, for all that, we couldn't predict it. Tom included. But I do believe that Tom really believed in and worked for a united Kenya and a united Africa. He often said publicly that unity didn't mean uniformity. He believed in unity in diversity, that is that people of different origins, religions, races and cultures were all human beings who could live together in harmony and shape their own destiny."

"One last question, Sir. Why do you think Mr Mboya was assassinated?" Wanjiku asked.

"If only I knew, young lady! If only I knew! I can't give you a precise reason but once again, with the wisdom of hindsight, I can attempt a possible one: Tom Mboya became a politician and politics is all about gaining and holding on to power. It is most likely that he made political enemies who felt that he stood in the way of their ambitions and decided that the only thing to do was to eliminate him altogether. We who remain can only speculate as to how he would have influenced Kenya had he lived to this day. And as young people like yourselves continue your researches, you will certainly get closer and closer to the truth."

Once again, Wanjiku and Lengai felt very special and important, as they did the rest of the time they spent with Mr Wamalwa, having tea and then going around his garden, before they left.

CHAPTER EIGHT

PROJECT ACCOMPLISHED:
COMING TO CONCLUSION

It was the final Saturday afternoon before the class presentations and Wanjiku had gone to Lengai's house. The two children were meeting to decide who was going to say what, exactly, when their turn came.

"Obviously, we're not going to be able to say everything we know in fifteen minutes," Wanjiku said.

"You're right," Lengai agreed.

"But you know something: My dad and I went on to the internet, just to confirm what Miss Ahmed had said about being spoilt for choice."

"Go on then," Wanjiku encouraged. "What happened?"

"My dad accessed an information search engine called Google," Lengai explained. "He typed in the name Tom Mboya and guess how many hits or references it had?"

Wanjiku thought of a large number: "Three thousand?"

"No, Wanjiku. You're not even close. About thirty thousand!"

"Wow!" Wanjiku said in disbelief.

"Yes, that's what I thought too," Lengai admitted. "But my dad explained that that included references to that name in all sorts of contexts and belonging to all sorts of people.

When he narrowed it down by typing in *"Tom Mboya Kenya History,"* the number of hits immediately decreased to about two thousand. Even then, you'd still have your work cut out for you ploughing through all those."

"You're telling me!" Wanjiku exclaimed.

"The internet is like a huge mansion with

innumerable rooms. You have to know where you're going to get about. Anyway, Miss Ahmed did advise us to steer clear of the internet for now. I think we've got enough to keep us going as it is. Since you came up with the time line information, you could spend a minute or two explaining Tom Mboya's place in the Africa of the times and the various struggles for independence and the dream of a United States of Africa. You could then go on to talk about his childhood and education and how they prepared him to be a nationalist and first highlighted his qualities as a gifted organiser and leader."

"Okay," Lengai accepted. "That's about half way. Then you could take over, Wanjiku, and talk about his influential roles as a trade unionist and politician, sadly leading to his assassination in the prime of his life. For all young people, you could stress that he was a disciplined learner who was always working to overcome his weaknesses and to improve his strengths. And, finally, you could mention the ways that we came up with this information, from scratch. Oh, yes! And whatever you do, don't forget to name your father as a hero of our researches!"

Both Wanjiku and Lengai laughed at that last remark. In any case, the two had every reason to be happy with themselves. They had worked hard, had helped each other to achieve their goals and they had had lots of fun in the process. In the end, they had learnt a lot. From then onwards, they would feel a particular attachment to Tom Mboya Street in Nairobi.

It had been a truly, exciting project, indeed!